D1632283

This book is due for return on or before the last date indicated
on label. Renewals may be obtained on application.

·814409
J

William Heinemann Ltd
Michelin House
81 Fulham Road
London SW3 6RB

LONDON · MELBOURNE · AUCKLAND

First published 1992
Text © Gene Kemp and Chantal Fouracre 1992
Illustrations © Carolyn Dinan 1992
ISBN 0 434 97690 3

Produced by Mandarin
Printed in Hong Kong

A school pack of BANANA BOOKS 49-54 is
available from Heinemann Educational Books
ISBN 0 435 00108 6

Chapter One

BEN RAN, JACKET flapping, feet flying,
new trainers full of bounce. He jumped
down the last four steps from their flat,
pushed open the swing door that led to the
back of the shop and ran in.

'Mum, can I go to the pet shop?'

His mother stopped filling the apple
section.

'Yes, you can. But mind the road. Cross
carefully.'

Ben shot through the Fruit and
Vegetable shop, fizzing like a pop bottle,

dodging all the customers.

'Watch it, lad,' shouted Mr Mackensie, the owner, so Ben slowed down.

Once through the door he sped off to the shops, the supermarket, bank, post office, butchers, bakers, hairdressers. Then to his favourite, the pet shop, on the other side, across the road which Ben's mother worried about.

'I'm all right on my own,' Ben always said.

And he was. He was used to it. There'd only ever been him and his Mum. But he didn't want her to worry, so he always crossed with the green man.

The pet shop was busy. Ben elbowed his way through, past the tropical fish to the back of the shop where his favourites were.

'What about my sausages, then?' squawked a loud, rusty voice. Percy the

parrot, older than anything, sat on his
perch keeping an eye on things.

'Who's a pretty boy then?' he croaked,
flapping his wings.

Ben picked up a bit of bark and held it
close to him. Percy reached out, took it
with his claw and put it into his wicked
beak.

'Bye,' said Ben, moving on to the small cages standing in racks. Golden brown and white hamsters huddled, sleeping in three of them, and there were two cases of mice.

On the ground stood the bigger boxes with two rabbits and a guinea pig with crimpy fur. Two new cages stood on a higher shelf, and inside the cages five new furry animals.

Ben couldn't take his eyes off them. He'd never seen anything like them before. Bigger than mice, smaller than hamsters, balls of fluff with bright eyes and big back legs and tails, they were just great. Two were pale grey, two pure white and the other was smudgy black, a sooty ball of fur.

Ben put his little finger up to the bars of the cage. One of the little creatures scampered over and sniffed it, his nose

wrinkling. With his other hand Ben
scrabbled in his pocket. Surely he'd got
some bits and pieces in there. Yip. A
peanut. Quick as a flash he pushed it
inside the bars of the cage. The little black
animal put out his paws, like two little
hands, took the peanut, sat up on his hind
legs and nibbled it.

When he'd finished he dropped down
to four legs, turned and ran across the cage
to the water bowl, back legs going
thumpety thump, thumpety thump,

thumpety thump.

Ben wanted that little black creature more than he'd wanted anything in the whole of his life. He stood there, watching it, its bright eyes, its fluffy fur, its little legs, its big tail. He was pleased that it had taken the nut and not been afraid of him.

'I want you, little black creature,' he whispered through the bars.

Slam! The door banged shut and a gang of noisy kids rushed through the shop. They pushed and shoved, nearly knocking Ben over, talking, yelling, laughing, arguing, as if he wasn't there. They swept Ben along with them until he ended up right at the back of the shop.

When he'd got back to the cage, the shop assistant was sticking a label on it.

NEW
COLOURED GERBILS
£5 each.

Ben's heart sank. He couldn't believe it. To get one he'd have to save for ages. He'd need lots of pocket money. He must manage somehow to find five pounds, BEFORE SOMEONE ELSE BOUGHT HIM.

At tea time he told his Mum all about the gerbil.

'You see, Mum, he's just perfect. All black and furry and clever. He'd be happy with me. I'd do all the cleaning out – honest!'

'It's not just that. There's the cage and the bedding and food as well as the gerbil. It's a bit much just now. We'll see about it later. Perhaps for your birthday . . . '

'But that's ages . . . '

'Ben, I can't manage it now. You'll have to be patient. I'm sorry,' said his mother. 'They'll have lots more gerbils in the shop.'

'But not that one. Not that little black gerbil.'

Ben choked back the tears.

* * * * *

That night in bed he thought about the little gerbil so hard and so long that as he drifted off to sleep he could feel the pitter patter of feet across the counterpane, a small furry creature curled up in the crook of his elbow.

He fell asleep trying out names.

'Smudge, or Blackie, or Jet . . . Whisper . . . or . . . Thumper . . . zz . . . zzz.'

Somehow or other he had to have that little black gerbil.

Chapter Two

'BEN BEAM! LIVES in a dream!' called
out Jimmy Todd and Kevin Spears as Ben
made his way into school. He didn't hear
them. Not even the school falling down
could have stopped him daydreaming
about the little black gerbil.

Ben imagined him tucked up in his
pocket, the small warm body next to his
side. He planned a day at school for a
(special) black gerbil.

Before School
Smuggle gerbil into desk with bedding,

food and water in a cut-off yoghurt cup.

After Assembly

Check on his safety. (He'd probably be curled up asleep in between his lunch box and pencil case!)

Playtime

Give him a run in the classroom. Simon and Penny (his friends) would be amazed at the trust the gerbil placed in him. Even Todd and Spears would shut up when he showed off his tricks!

He was planning to take his pet into "Singing Together" (tucked up in the end of his tie) when he bumped into Miss Tanner and knocked the pile of song books to the floor.

'Ben Beam! Wake up!' she exclaimed.

Ben mumbled sorry and picked up the books. Miss Tanner helped.

Together they made their way to the classroom.

The class were doing a Project on Animals. They'd made folders on horses, cats, dogs, monkeys, elephants, tigers and all endangered species, even sharks and poisonous jellyfish. Art was Ben's favourite subject, and he'd begun a big picture of a lion. But he left it and started a new picture, a picture of a little black gerbil.

'Hiya!' said Simon, who sat next to

him. Ben took no notice.

'Hey! Guess what . . . ' Simon began
again.

'QUIET,' said Miss Tanner, trying to
take the register.

'I've got a rabbit!' hissed Simon. 'Dad
bought it!'

Ben's happy dream-bubble burst. Why
should Simon have a rabbit? It wasn't
fair!

Even if he saved every penny he got, it would take weeks before he could buy the gerbil. By then it would have gone for sure. While Simon had his rabbit.

Ben hated Simon. And his rabbit.

It was a long, draggy day. Simon told

everyone over and over again about the rabbit. A crowd of kids was going round to see it after school and Ben was also invited but he invented an excuse and ran out on his own.

Quicker than quick, he rushed to the pet shop, scared stiff that the gerbil might already have been sold. As he went he sang under his breath,

'If I don't . . . tread on the cracks . . . he'll be there . . . he'll be there . . . he'll be there.'

Vroom! In at the door of the pet shop straight into a stomach with a very fat man behind it.

'Look where you're going!' the man cried.

But Ben only had eyes for THE CAGE. Was he there or had somebody bought him? He couldn't see him. He must have gone! Oh, no! PANIC! PANIC!

But there he was. Black, furry, fantastic! Suddenly he stretched up on his back legs like a tiny kangaroo. Ben loved him, wanted him as much as ever. He must have him for his own. All he needed was the money to buy him. But how was he to get five pounds? And the rest for the cage and a wheel, the bedding and the food. What Ben needed was to find treasure!

Thinking hard he wandered out of the door. Treasure troves didn't seem likely but he could do jobs for people. And he'd save his pocket money, to add to what there was in his money box. If he didn't tread on the cracks in the pavement it would be all right, he'd get enough money. He bounced along the pavement dodging the cracks.

Something gleamed in one of those cracks, something round, something bright and shiny.

Ben bent down to pick it up.

Treasure!

A beautiful new pound coin. He looked round. No one was near him. No one was looking for a pound coin on the pavement.

'I think I can keep it,' thought Ben and he put it in his pocket.

'Hey, that's mine. Hand it over, it's all I've got till next week.' A mum with a double buggy popped out of nowhere holding out her hand. For a minute Ben thought of running away. Then slowly, with a deep sigh, he gave her the coin.

All the way home he went on looking in the pavement cracks, but all he found was a lolly stick and a safety pin.

Chapter Three

AND WHO SHOULD be waiting at home
but his Grandma.

'Got any jobs for me,' he burst out,
panting hard, not even saying 'Hello.'

'I . . . don't . . . know, Ben,' she
answered, surprised. 'Why? Is it Job
Week or something?'

'No, it's just that I want to buy a little
black gerbil. And Mum says we haven't
got 'nuff money '-cause of the bills and
everything.'

'Well . . . you can go and fetch me the

evening paper. And some peppermints.
You know the ones I like. Here's the
money.'

'Goodness me. Did you go by space
shuttle?' Grandma asked five minutes
later, but Ben was panting too hard to
answer. Gran took the paper and
peppermints from him and handed over
some coins. 'Here. This'll help towards
whatever it is you want.'

Ben ran to his bedroom and counted up
his money. It still wasn't enough.

He bounced round next door and rang the bell and Mrs Crockett answered, a big lady, rather grand but always kind to Ben.

'Any jobs?' he asked. 'Please,' he added. He'd done jobs for her before. She couldn't let him down this time, could she?

'All right. I'm sorting out rubbish in the kitchen. Bottles go here for the bottle

bank. The newspapers in a pile here for re-
cycling. The rest go in this bag. I've been
turning out my son's room. He's grown-
up now and getting rid of all his old stuff.
You can have those comics if you like.'

'Oh, great,' said Ben, but he was *really*
looking to see if there was anything for a
little black gerbil.

His eyes were so busy searching that
they didn't see an old tin of paint which
hadn't got its lid on properly. Ben
knocked it over and it rolled. Out oozed
squelchy dirty-white paint all over the
rubbish and onto the kitchen floor.

'Oh, Ben!' said Mrs Crockett, then,
'No, don't worry, you couldn't help it.
Never mind, I'll finish off here.'

'Wait,' said Mrs Crockett.

Ben waited.

'What about this? I think it's too good
to throw away, but my son doesn't want it

any more. Would you like it?'

IT was a large cage with little stairs leading to *two* upstairs rooms, a wheel and two little bowls. An unused packet of pet food stood inside it.

'Would I like it?' Ben cried. 'You can bet your life I'd like it.'

'Yippee!' he shouted as he carried the cage home. 'All I need now is THE LITTLE BLACK GERBIL!'

Chapter Four

NEXT DAY, AFTER school dinner, Ben hurried back to his classroom to finish his gerbil picture. It was on Miss Tanner's desk. Next to it stood two untidy piles of exercise books and lying between them like a little animal lay a fat leather purse. It was open and Ben found he was looking at a five pound note.

'Gerbil money,' he thought and the little black creature danced round and round in his head.

Footsteps ran up behind him and faster

than a streaky fox Jimmy Todd popped up at his side.

'Naughty, naughty! Teachers shouldn't leave money lying around,' he grinned. 'We'd better put it into her bag.'

Jimmy's fingers were quick and nimble.

'There – that's it,' he said and shot away.

Ben tidied up the books, picked up his picture and went to his desk. He would

never really have taken the money,
however much he wanted the little black
gerbil.

* * *

Miss Tanner was pleased that he'd
tidied up the books for her.

'I was in such a rush. Thank you, Ben.'

Miss Tanner told her class she was
pleased with them.

Later she told them she was not pleased

with them and had another talk, this time about respecting other people's property, and how wrong it was to steal.

You see, the five pound note had gone. It wasn't in the fat leather purse any more.

'We didn't take it, Miss,' said Simon.

'It was with the books, I know,' said a sad Miss Tanner to the Headmaster, who had arrived. 'I had to rush off and leave it all for a minute,' she added.

'Miss, Ben Beam tidied your books,' said Jimmy Todd.

26

'Oh, Ben!' said Miss Tanner.

Ben jumped up. 'It wasn't me. It wasn't!'

'Ben wouldn't do a thing like that!' shouted Simon.

'QUIET! Come with me, Ben. We'll talk about it in my office,' said the Headmaster.

Ben stumbled out of the classroom past all the staring faces. He wanted to cry. He felt awful.

At the end of school time, a subdued Ben walked home. He didn't want to go to the pet shop or even think about his gerbil. The awful events of the day still crowded in his head. The terrible unfairness of it all. He hadn't stolen the money. What was the point of wanting his little black gerbil when everything was against him, when everything went wrong.

He couldn't forget how the Headmaster had spoken about truth and honesty, about not stealing things and all the time he, Ben, *was* telling the truth!

It was the school caretaker who saved the day. Luckily for Ben he'd been cleaning the windows and he had seen another lad at the teacher's desk, touching things. That red-haired one, Johnny? or Jimmy? he explained. He knew Ben hadn't taken the note.

Ben was glad that the caretaker had
seen, and glad that Sir made Jimmy
confess. And the five pound note turned
up in an exercise book where Jimmy had
put it for fun!

Chapter Five

WHEN BEN REACHED home he felt too
tired to bother with anything much. He
just wanted his bed, his books and toys,
his own safe room around him. He lay
down, his face buried in his pillow.
'Where have the happy times gone?' he
thought to himself and then, 'Do I even
want the little black gerbil? *Really* want
him like before?' He pictured the little
creature, its brightness and alertness
stirring him. Suddenly Ben knew that he
had to see him again.

'Even if I can't buy him, I can still see him each day at the shop!' he thought, and he tipped his money onto the bed, scooped it up and ran out of his room and into the street.

'Watch out, Ben!' gasped Grandma as Ben bumped into her and fell down. She helped him up and hugged him.

'Grandma,' said Ben, quietly.

She looked at him closely. 'You look a bit pale and worn out. Here, have a bit of extra pocket money to cheer you up,' and she gave Ben a one pound coin.

For Ben, the sun shone again. 'Thank you, Grandma, so much,' he said and hugged her hard.

He could buy the gerbil. Hip hip hip hooray. He could buy it today. Today was Gerbil Day!

'Here I come,' he thought, running into the pet shop and straight to the cage.

His heart stopped. The cage was empty.

It was quite bare. The little black gerbil had gone. All the gerbils had gone.

Chapter Six

'I'M WORRIED ABOUT Ben,' said his
Mum to Miss Tanner.

'Why, what's the matter? Is he ill or
something?'

'No, he's not ill. But he's got no interest
in anything at all. As soon as he comes
home from school he goes and lies on the
bed. It's not like him at all. I'll have to take
him to the doctor.'

But the doctor said there was nothing
wrong with Ben.

One day, Ben started helping at the pet

shop. When he'd finished he asked Mr Biddle if he'd got any more gerbils coming in.

'Not at the moment,' said Mr Biddle. 'But if you come in and help me now and then you'll be able to keep your eyes open for them, won't you?'

So Ben did. Almost every afternoon he went and helped at the pet shop. Sometimes gerbils appeared in the cages but never a black one. The end of term came and school finished. Ben enjoyed being with the animals. The hamsters and mice grew to know and trust him. They didn't scuttle away when Ben cleared out their cages, but snuffled up to his hand and took treats from him.

Mr Biddle liked to have Ben helping him and said that the world needed more people like him caring for animals unselfishly.

One evening, at the start of the holidays, Mr Biddle seemed sad. When Ben asked why, he took him to the back corner, and there curled up in an open topped box was the smallest baby gerbil Ben had ever seen – all alone lying still, eyes closed, its soft black downy fur just growing.

'A friend brought him in today,' he said. 'A cat got the mother and the others.

35

But I haven't time to feed him every two hours, that's the trouble.'

'I have,' said Ben. 'I've got time.'

Mr Biddle smiled. 'Come on, then. I'll show you what to do, lad. Keep the box in a warm spot and feed him every two to three hours in the daytime. At night one feed will do. Will your mother let you feed him at night?'

'I'll keep him in the bedroom,' said Ben.

Mr Biddle showed Ben how to feed the little creature with a dispenser for putting drops into sore ears.

'If you save this one you can have him,' he said. 'But you mustn't mind if he dies. Sometimes they do, you know.'

'Not this one,' thought Ben as he left the shop, holding the box with extra special care.

At home he held out the box for his

Mum to see.

'Poor little thing,' she said.

The little black gerbil lay there, hardly breathing.

'We'll try,' she said.

But it seemed as if trying wasn't enough. The little black gerbil would not drink the milk.

'It's too small to live,' thought Ben. 'Oh, little gerbil, please don't die.' He watched the creature closely. Noticed its tiny sealed eyes, its fragile naked limbs and small curled round body showing pinky-blue through the fur. Tears trickled down Ben's face. 'Keep breathing, keep breathing,' he thought.

Suddenly he had an idea. He knew baby puppies liked warmth and security.

'Mum! Let's warm him up with a hot water bottle!' he cried.

Quickly his Mum fetched a hot water bottle with a furry cover. Ben made a hollow in it with his fist and they laid the little creature in it. After a moment the gerbil wriggled and feebly kicked its legs. It liked the fur and the warmth.

'Try now!' said Mum.

Carefully Ben pushed the feeder into the tiny mouth and squeezed a drop. Amazingly the gerbil swallowed, its mouth and throat muscles working. Ben did it again, and again the milk went down. Ben smiled.

Two hours later Ben fed him again and again, and then again and again, and each time the little black gerbil DRANK SOME MORE!

At last his Mum sent him to bed. But it was difficult to get to sleep. Would the little black gerbil still be alive in the morning? Would he be there for Ben to talk to, to hold, to watch, to feed each day when he came home from school?

Chapter Seven

BEN RUNS, JACKET flapping, feet flying, new trainers full of bounce. He pushes open the swing door and springs up the stairs two at a time.

He runs into the flat and into his own room where a cage stands on his chest of drawers.

'Tch . . . tch . . . tch,' calls Ben in their secret language.

'Tch . . . tch,' and from the nest box out wriggles a furry black gerbil. With bright beady eyes looking at Ben, he runs

thumpety, thumpety across the cage and
in a moment boy and gerbil are playing
happily.

Just as always the little gerbil runs up Ben's arm and sits on his shoulder where he scutches his fur up and waits. Just as always Ben gives him a peanut and, balancing on back legs, he holds it in his front paws to eat it.

He is just a little black gerbil after all. Just a little black furry animal that belongs to a boy.